Lost in the Fog

Story by Cameron Macintosh
Illustrations by Wendy Tan Shiau Wei

Contents

Chapter 1

Fun in the Snow

Ida and her mum were staying
with Gran and Poppa.
Ida's grandparents lived in the country.
Their cabin was near a high hill.

Ida had been waiting for snow to fall all week.
At last, there was deep snow on the ground.
She could ride her sled down the hill!

Ida and Mum climbed to the top of the hill. They took turns to slide down the hill on their sleds.

Ida and Mum each went up and down three times.

Chapter 2

A Cloud of Fog

They had climbed up the hill once more,
when Ida said, "Look, Mum!
There is some fog coming our way."

Mum turned and saw a big cloud of fog
slowly rolling towards the hill.
"We had better go back
to Gran and Poppa's house," she said.

"Quick, let's go down now," said Ida.
"I'll go first!"

Ida sat on her sled
and started sliding down the hill.
As she slid, a wind blew the fog even closer.

Ida slowly came to a stop in a field of snow
by the hill.

Just as Ida stood up, the fog rolled down the hill and across the field.

Soon, the fog was so thick
that Ida could only see
two or three steps ahead of her.

"Mum!" she called loudly.

Ida could hear Mum's voice
coming from the top of the hill,
but she couldn't work out
what Mum was saying.

Ida picked up the rope of her sled
and started to walk back up the hill,
towards Mum.

By now, it was very hard to see
through the fog.

Ida began to feel scared.
She couldn't tell which way she was facing.

It was cold in the fog, too.
Ida began to shiver.

Chapter 3

Ida's Red Scarf

Ida called out to Mum again,
but Mum didn't call back to her.

Suddenly, Ida remembered
that she was wearing a red scarf.
She pulled the scarf out from the top of her jacket.
Then, she started waving it in the air above her head.

A minute later, Ida heard Mum's voice.

"I can see your scarf!" Mum called.
"Stay there, Ida. I'm coming to you now."

Soon, Ida saw Mum coming towards her through the fog.
She rushed over to Mum
and gave her a big hug.

"Are you all right?" asked Mum.

"Yes," said Ida. "I got lost.
But then I remembered I had my scarf on.
It is red, so I knew it would be easy for you
to see it in the fog."

"It was very clever of you
to wave your scarf around," said Mum.
"I could see you when I came down the hill."

"Thanks, Mum," said Ida.
"Now, I think it's time for some hot chocolate with Gran and Poppa!"